ROCKS AND MINERALS
THE WORLD BENEATH OUR FEET

Written by Gail Saunders-Smith

STECK-VAUGHN

A Harcourt Company

www.steck-vaughn.com

Contents

Minerals: More Than We Can Imagine

Minerals make our life possible. We use them at work and at play. We wear them and even eat them. Chalk is a mineral. So is the aluminum in aluminum foil. But what exactly is a mineral? A **mineral** is a natural solid material that is not made of living things. The particles of a mineral are arranged in a repeating pattern. This pattern creates a **crystal,** so all minerals are made of one or more crystals.

About 3600 different minerals can be found on Earth. Each mineral contains one or more of the 92 **elements** in Earth's crust. Most minerals are made from their own special recipe of elements. For example, salt is made of two elements. Some minerals, such as aluminum, gold, and diamond, are made of only one element. Some minerals, such as gold, are metals. Others are not.

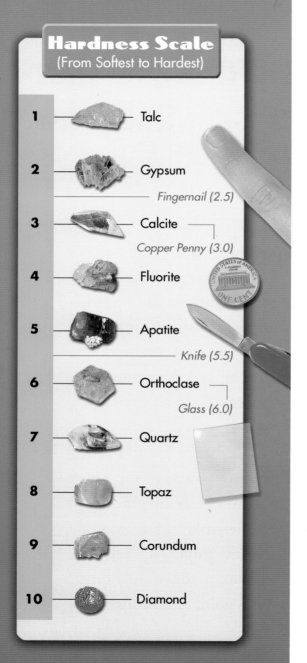

Hardness Scale
(From Softest to Hardest)

1	Talc
2	Gypsum
	Fingernail (2.5)
3	Calcite
	Copper Penny (3.0)
4	Fluorite
5	Apatite
	Knife (5.5)
6	Orthoclase
	Glass (6.0)
7	Quartz
8	Topaz
9	Corundum
10	Diamond

Some minerals look alike. Scientists use special tests to tell them apart. One test is for hardness. Hardness is measured by how difficult it is to scratch the mineral. In 1822 Fredrich Mohs created a scale. His scale lists common minerals, from softest to hardest. Mohs numbered the minerals from 1 to 10. Number 1 is the easiest to scratch. Number 10 is the most difficult to scratch. Each mineral can be used to scratch the minerals that are softer than it.

Another way to tell minerals apart is by how they look. Some minerals have **luster**. Luster is the way light bounces off a mineral. A mineral's luster can be dull, metallic (like metal), pearly, glassy, greasy, or silky. Some minerals are clear. Light passes right through them.

Scientists can also tell some minerals apart by their color. Just looking at a mineral's color can be confusing, though. Lots of minerals are white or clear. Some come in several different colors. Experts have a better way to test a mineral's color than just by looking. They rub the mineral against a rough tile. The mineral leaves a streak of powder on the tile. The color of a mineral's streak is always the same.

Quartz is a very useful mineral. It is used in radios, watches, and microphones. Quartz comes in different colors, too. Purple quartz is known as amethyst (AM uh thist). It is used in jewelry.

Minerals come in many different colors.

Most minerals don't have a smell. A few, though, give off an odor when they are heated. One mineral smells like horseradish. Clay gives off an odd smell when it is sprayed with hot water.

It's a bad idea to put minerals in our mouth. However, some minerals do leave a taste on the tongue. Some are sour, bitter, or even sweet. Salt is a mineral we eat every day. It makes our food taste better. We also need it to be healthy.

Some minerals can do very strange things. Magnetite is a natural magnet. A few kinds of minerals carry an electric charge. A few glow in the dark. Some fizz when an acid is placed on them.

Rocks: As Old as the Hills

When minerals stick together, they make rocks. There are only three kinds of rocks. These three kinds of rocks have been around as long as Earth itself. They are being made this very minute. Rocks are being broken down. The minerals in them are forming new rocks.

Igneous Rock

Igneous rock starts out as magma. Magma is thick, gooey melted rock. It is found deep inside the Earth. Sometimes magma oozes out of cracks in rocks beneath the ocean. Other times it spews out from a volcano. Then it flows down the volcano's sides. When magma reaches Earth's surface, it is called **lava.**

Magma usually forms crystals as it cools into rock. When magma cools slowly, it makes a kind of rock called basalt (buh SAWLT). Basalt has small crystal grains. When magma cools quickly, crystals do not have time to form.

Types of igneous rock. Clockwise from left: obsidian, granite, and basalt.

Lava that cools quickly makes a rock called obsidian (uhb SID ee uhn). Obsidian is usually black or brown. It has sharp edges. It was used long ago to make tools such as knives and arrowheads.

Sometimes flowing lava has foam on top. The foam hardens into a kind of rock called pumice (PUHM is). The gas bubbles in the foam become holes in the rock. Pumice is so light that it can float on water. It is often used to scrub away stains.

Magma that cools slowly deep inside the Earth forms granite (GRAN it). Slow cooling helps large crystals to form. The crystals can be seen easily with the naked eye. Granite is often found in the cores of mountain chains. Granite is a strong, pretty stone that polishes well.

Sedimentary Rock

Sedimentary rock is formed when layers of **sediment** press together. Sediment is tiny bits of gravel, sand, mud, dead animals, animal waste, and leaves. These things lie at the bottom of lakes, rivers, and seas. As sediment stacks up, the bottom layers are squashed. Minerals in the water help glue the sediment together.

One of the most common kinds of sedimentary rock is sandstone. The Grand Canyon in Arizona cuts through many layers of sandstone. The Colorado River slowly wore the rock away. The Rocky Mountains are also made of sandstone. Huge pieces of the rock folded to make ridges. Ayers Rock in Australia is a big chunk of reddish sandstone. The stone circle in England called Stonehenge is made from giant blocks of sandstone.

Types of sedimentary rock. Left to right: sandstone, coal, and conglomerate.

Rocks were used to make the first paints. Long ago, people crushed brightly colored rocks. Then they mixed the powder with animal fat.

Limestone is one type of sedimentary rock. It is made of layers of shells and tiny plants. The shells and plants pile up over millions of years. Limestone is usually white.

Metamorphic Rock

Igneous rock and sedimentary rock sometimes change into **metamorphic rock.** The rock is heated and squeezed very hard. Marble is the best-known type of metamorphic rock. It is made from limestone. The limestone is squeezed until only the crystals are left.

Marble cuts easily and polishes nicely. Sculptors from all ages have used marble to make statues. The famous sculptor Michelangelo used Italian marble. Beautiful buildings are also built of marble.

Types of metamorphic rock. Clockwise from left: marble, mica, and quartzite.

Metals: Hard as Rocks?

When people discovered metals, life on Earth took a giant leap forward. Metals last a long, long time. They carry electricity and heat. They can be bent or molded into almost any shape. Most metals are found in rocks. Rocks that contain metals are called **ores.**

The first metals that humans found were gold, silver, and copper. Gold and copper were discovered about 8000 years ago. People shaped gold into jewelry and other beautiful things. They hammered copper into weapons and tools. Around 6000 years ago, people melted tin and copper and mixed them together to make a metal called **bronze.** It is much harder than copper. It makes better weapons and tools. About 3000 years ago, humans discovered iron. People learned that a very hot fire could melt this new metal out of certain rocks. Iron is even stronger than bronze. People used iron to make many new things.

Every day, metals help us eat, drink, travel, have fun, and even learn. Juice and soda come in aluminum cans. Airplanes are built of strong, light titanium (ty TAN ee uhm). Tungsten is added to steel to make it harder. We have also discovered new metals. Still, nothing can quite take the place of gold, silver, and copper.

Gold

Gold is a **precious** metal. It is not just beautiful. It is also quite strong and does not **tarnish.** Gold has a bright yellow color. It can be highly polished. Gold is found in **veins** inside quartz rock. Miners dig the gold out of these veins. Sometimes wind

Gold is used to make the face shields of astronauts' helmets.

and water wear away rock with gold in it. Then little pebbles, or **nuggets,** of gold are left behind. The nuggets are washed into rivers and creeks. Some people use pans to search rivers and streams for gold.

The mercury in old-fashioned thermometers comes from an ore called cinnabar. The metal it holds is very strange. Mercury melts at a very low temperature. At room temperature it is a liquid. Because mercury is poisonous, so is cinnabar.

Most gold bits are too small to see. The biggest pure gold nugget was found in Australia in 1869. It weighed 156 pounds (71 kilograms). Gold nuggets found in California started the California Gold Rush in 1849.

Silver

Silver is used to make knives, forks, and other eating utensils.

Silver is also a precious metal. It has a bright silver-white color. Oxygen in the air makes it tarnish. By itself, silver is not very strong. It must be mixed with another metal. Most silver comes from mines in Mexico. Silver has been mined in Mexico since the year 1500. Silver is also found in Russia and Peru. It is usually found in large nuggets or grains. Silver is also found in tree-shaped clusters or twisted strands.

Of all the metals, silver is the best carrier of heat and electricity. It is used in many types of **industry.** Beautiful coins and jewelry are also made from silver.

Platinum

Platinum is the rarest and most valuable precious metal. It does not tarnish. Platinum melts only at a very high temperature. Most acids can't harm it. Platinum is very soft. It is used to make jewelry. It is also used to make tooth fillings. Platinum usually forms in igneous rocks. The grains of metal in the rock are too small to see.

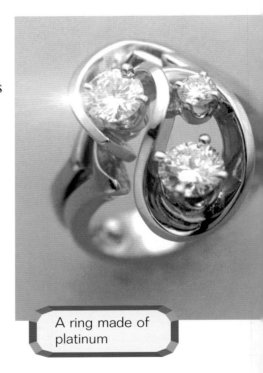

A ring made of platinum

Gold and silver can be melted out of the rock around it. The rock around platinum must be removed with chemicals. These chemicals were not known until modern times. For this reason, platinum was not used until the 1800s.

Copper

Copper is a useful metal. It is stronger and harder than gold. It is found naturally in tree-like clusters or twisted strands. Sometimes it is taken from other ores. Copper is reddish in color. It is used to make pipes, wires, and many other goods.

Giant spools of copper wire

Gems: Nature's Sparklers

The most beautiful minerals are called gemstones, or **gems.** A gem is a mineral that can be used in jewelry after it is cut and polished. Many gems are made into jewelry. Some gems aren't good enough for jewelry. They are used in industry.

Some gems form about 100 miles (161 kilometers) deep within the Earth. Minerals there are heated or squeezed into gems. Jade and garnet are made in this way. Most gems are dug out of the Earth in mines. Volcanoes throw out a few gems. Underground streams wash up a few more. The most precious gems are rubies and emeralds. They are precious because they have rare crystal shapes. These gems form in only a few places on Earth.

Part of a gem's color comes from how it takes in light. Minerals inside the gem also help give it color. Different minerals can turn the same kind of gem different colors. Most gems are very small. They are weighed in **carats.** One carat equals one fifth of a gram.

Diamonds

Diamonds are the hardest of all gemstones. A diamond can only be scratched by another diamond. The word *diamond* comes from a Latin word that means "hard." Most diamonds don't have any color. A few diamonds are yellow, pink, blue, green, brown, gray, and even black.

Diamonds are mined all over the world. They are found in long, skinny rock shapes. These shapes are called "pipes." They go straight down for about 50 miles (80 kilometers). Some diamonds have been found sitting on the ground or in streams. Today most diamonds come from Australia.

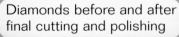
Diamonds before and after final cutting and polishing

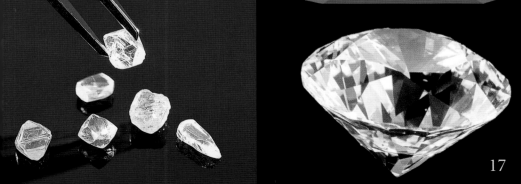

Most diamonds that are dug up are used in industry. Because they are so hard, diamonds are good for cutting and grinding. Diamond-tipped drills can cut through almost anything.

The biggest white diamond ever found is called the Cullinan Diamond. It was dug up in South Africa in 1905. It weighed more than 3000 carats. That's about 21 ounces (595 grams)! The Cullinan Diamond was cut into smaller gems. The next-largest white diamond, the Excelsior, was also found in South Africa. It weighs 995.20 carats. The biggest yellow diamond weighs 128.51 carats. It was found in South Africa's Kimberly Mine in 1878. The Hope Diamond is the largest blue diamond. It weighs 45.5 carats.

The Hope Diamond

Rubies, Sapphires, and Emeralds

Rubies, sapphires, and emeralds are made of corundum (kohr UHN duhm). By itself, corundum is clear. When different metals are mixed with corundum, it turns different colors. The results are rubies, sapphires, and emeralds.

Ruby

Sapphire

Some rubies and sapphires have tiny slivers of another mineral inside them. The slivers make a white, six-sided star shape in the middle of the gem. These are called star rubies and star sapphires. They are cut with a smooth top to show off the star inside.

Rubies are the second-hardest stone. They are usually found in metamorphic or igneous rock. A few rubies are found as pebbles in streams and rivers.

Emerald

Opals

Opals are strange-looking gems. Light dances on their surface. The light makes a rainbow of colors. White opals are called milk opals. Red ones are called fire opals. Clear opals are called water opals. The most precious opals are black opals.

A water opal

Opals are different from other kinds of gemstones. They are softer than most other gems, so they scratch easily. Opals have no crystals, so they are not minerals. They form in sedimentary rock in dry places. Opals can take the place of bone, wood, and shell in fossils. They can also form in veins in igneous rock. Opals actually have water inside them. Over time, opals may dry out or crack. Dry opals are not very pretty. Most opals are found in Australia.

Turquoise

Turquoise was one of the first gems ever mined. Iron and copper make turquoise blue, green, or even gray. Turquoise forms in dry places. American Indians use turquoise to make jewelry and works of art. Like opals, turquoise is not a true mineral. It cracks and breaks easily. The color of turquoise can be changed by heat. Temperatures higher than 480° F (250° C) turn turquoise an ugly green.

Turquoise

Aquamarine, a blue-green gem, is often baked to make it darker. People heat light-colored gems to about 800° F (426° C). At this heat, the gems' color changes to a darker blue.

Gems

Amethyst
Common color: purple

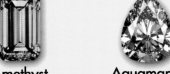
Aquamarine
Common colors: blue, violet

Diamond
Common colors: colorless, green, blue, black, yellow, brown, pink

Emerald
Common color: green

Garnet
Common colors: red, violet, green

Opal
Common colors: mixed, yellow-brown

Peridot
Common color: green

Ruby
Common colors: red, pink

Sapphire
Common colors: blue, green, yellow, pink

Topaz
Common colors: blue, green, brown, red, pink, yellow

Tourmaline
Common colors: red, blue, purple, brown, green, and many others

Turquoise
Common colors: blue, violet, green

Organics: Once Alive, Now Gems

Some of the most interesting gems were once parts of living creatures. These gems are called organic gems, or **organics.** Pearls, amber, jet, and coral are all organics.

Pearls

Pearls are the most valuable organic gems. Pearls are formed by shellfish in warm water. A grain of sand or other tiny object gets trapped inside the shell.

A pearl

At first the animal tries to wash out the object. If that doesn't work, the animal covers the object with a smooth material. This material is called **nacre.** Layer after layer of shiny nacre builds up over the object. In about seven years, the object is a pearl. Most pearls are small. They range from less than $\frac{1}{16}$ inch (2 millimeters) to about 2 inches (5 centimeters) around. Pearls can be white, pink, green, blue, brown, or black. Different

22

shellfish make different colors of pearls. The temperature of the water can also affect the color of pearls. Like snowflakes, no two pearls are exactly the same.

Amber

Amber looks like a clear mineral. In fact, it is the sap of pine trees that lived long ago. Over time, the sap hardened into a fossil. Sometimes plants or animals got stuck in the sap. When the sap turned to amber, they were trapped inside. Leaves, pine needles, insects, and spiders

Amber containing an insect

have been found in amber. Some amber even holds small frogs and lizards. Amber with plants or animals inside is worth a lot of money. Scientists think the oldest amber ever found is about 100 million years old.

23

Amber is golden-yellow or golden-orange. When it is found, it usually looks cracked or dull. When it is polished, it looks smooth and clear. Some pieces of amber weigh as much as 18 pounds (8 kilograms). If amber is rubbed, it gets an electric charge. The electricity draws dust. Amber can also be lit with a fire. It gives off a sweet smell as it burns.

Long ago people used amber for medicine. They also melted it down to make varnish. Now amber is mostly used to make jewelry.

Jet

Jet is sometimes called black amber. Like amber, it makes electricity when rubbed, and it has been used as medicine. People of long ago ground up the

Jet

jet. Then they sprinkled it in water or wine. Jet looks dull until it is cut and polished. Then it becomes a beautiful brown or black gem.

Some people put jet and coal in the same group. They are both made mostly of carbon. But unlike coal, jet doesn't form under the ground. Scientists think that jet forms in the ocean. They think tree trunks sink into the mud at the ocean bottom. The wood is pressed together and becomes jet. In the 1800s, people who had lost a loved one wore jet jewelry. They thought the black color of jet matched their sad feelings.

Coral

Coral is made from the skeletons of tiny ocean animals. Coral is found in warm water near seashores. These animals live in groups called colonies. The colonies branch out like small bushes. The colonies slowly build large coral reefs. Divers harvest coral from the reefs.

Coral can be red, pink, white, or blue. Some coral is black or golden. Red coral is the most valuable. Coral is easy

An earring containing pink coral

to break, and its color may fade over time. People once gave coral to young children. They thought coral could keep the children safe.

Fossils: Between a Rock and a Hard Place

Fossils are windows into the past. Insects trapped in amber are fossils. So are shells trapped in limestone. Other fossils include prints made by plants and animals on rocks. The footprints of animals are fossils, too. So are **petrified** trees.

Most fossils are found in sedimentary rocks. Plants and animals became trapped in mud or tar and died. Over time the plants' and animals' soft parts rotted away. The hard parts, like shells, bones, teeth, and stems, were left. As the years passed, the sediment that held the animal or plant hardened into rock. Very slowly, even the hard parts of the plants and animals rotted away. Minerals filled in the spaces they left. These hard parts were petrified, or turned to stone. A fossil might be shaped like a shell, but it is really a rock.

Petrified Forests

Around 200 million years ago, a logjam of trees floated down a river. In what is now Arizona, they got stuck in sand and mud. Over many years, the trees petrified. Some of the trees turned into opal.

Arizona's Petrified Forest

The petrified trees still look like wood. Some of the trees still have growth rings. Large groups of fossil trees are called petrified forests.

Other Plant Fossils

Other plant fossils can be found near beds of coal and in sedimentary rock. Fossils of whole plants are hard to find. Most fossils only show part of a leaf or stem. Plant fossils are often found in sandstone near the beds of dry rivers and streams.

Fern fossils

27

A fish fossil

Fish Fossils

Fish fossils are hard to find. Fish skeletons are not very strong. They usually break up before they can turn to stone. Shark teeth, though, are hard and bony. Many fossilized shark teeth have been found. Most fish fossils are found in rock such as shale and limestone.

Shell Fossils

An ammonite fossil

Oyster shells are thick. They make good fossils. Fossil oysters are easy to find. Often, though, only one part of the shell is found. This is because oysters' shells open when they die. Ammonite (AM uh nyt) shells are other common fossils. Ammonites lived in warm seas long ago. They had coiled shells with many chambers, or parts. Their fossils are usually found in limestone.

In 1811 twelve-year-old Mary Anning dug up the fossil skeleton of a sea creature near her home in Dorset, England. She later found many other types of fossils. The tongue twister "She sells seashells down by the seashore" was written about Mary Anning.

Space Rocks:
The Sky Is Falling

If we look carefully at the night sky, we might see a white light streak across it. The light looks like a star. In fact, it is only a falling space rock. Many of the rocks on Earth came from space. Some fell to Earth as **meteorites.** Astronauts have brought others home to study.

Meteorites

Throughout its history, space rocks called meteors have blasted the Earth. Most space rocks burn up as they rocket through the atmosphere. Some bigger chunks, however, make it through the atmosphere. We call these rocks meteorites. About 22,000 meteorites hit the Earth every year! Most of them fall in the ocean or on land where there are no people.

There are three kinds of meteorites: stony, iron, and stony-iron. Stony meteorites are the most common.

The Grootfontein Meteorite

They are made of minerals that are also found on Earth. Some stony meteorites look like lava rocks. They are not as strong as lava rocks, though. The largest stony meteorite was found in Texas. It weighed 638 pounds (289 kilograms).

Stony-iron meteorites are rare. Earth's weather wears them away quickly. One of the largest stony-iron meteorites was found in Southwest Africa. It is called the Grootfontein Meteorite.

So far, about 21 meteorites from the moon have been found on Earth. One meteorite from the moon traveled around the Earth for nine million years before it landed in Antarctica.

In the 1980s two interesting meteorites were found in the Antarctic. Meteorite MAC88105 is from the moon. It matches the moon rocks brought back by astronauts. Meteorite ALH84001 is from Mars. The gases inside the meteorite match measurements of Mars' atmosphere. Scientists think the same comet or asteroid hit the moon and Mars and blew chunks of both into space. Some of the chunks fell to Earth.

Moon Rocks

Most moon rocks are about 4 million years old. Astronauts have brought about 840 pounds (380 kilograms) of rocks back to Earth from the moon.

Many of the rocks, like Rock 15016, are made of basalt. Basalt is common on Earth. It is an igneous rock with tiny holes made by gas bubbles. Moon rocks are also made of olivine (AH luh veen). Olivine is a familiar Earth mineral. Many of the moon rocks, like Rock 79135, are breccias (BREH kee uhz). These rocks are made of sharp pieces of other rocks. The soil on the moon is all crushed rock.

A meteorite from the moon

A meteorite from Mars

Mars Rocks

Mars is Earth's neighbor in space. It is covered with red dust. The red color comes from a form of iron that is also found on Earth. About 20 meteorites from Mars have been found on Earth. They usually have a dark crust. The crust forms when the outside of the rock melts in Earth's atmosphere. The most famous meteorite from Mars is shaped like a potato. Odd chains of crystals were found inside it. Some scientists thought these crystals showed that tiny animals once lived on Mars.

NASA plans to send a robot to Mars in 2011 or 2013. The robot will bring back rocks to study. The project will cost $1 to $2 billion. Scientists hope the rocks will tell us more about Mars.

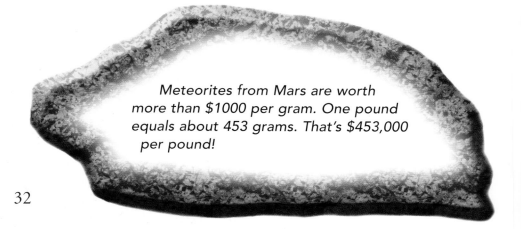

Meteorites from Mars are worth more than $1000 per gram. One pound equals about 453 grams. That's $453,000 per pound!

Fooling with Mother Nature

Nature makes pretty things. People have learned how to do many of the things nature can do. People can even make fake gems, minerals, and fossils.

Pearls

Man-made pearls are called cultured pearls. They are hard to tell from natural pearls. Even though cultured pearls are pretty, they are less valuable than natural ones. To make a pearl, people put a small bead inside a live oyster. Over about four years, the oyster builds a pearl around it. The oysters live in special underwater cages.

A pearl necklace

Amber

Amber is easy to fake. Man-made **resin** or plastic can be made to look like amber. Some people cover real insects with plastic. Others press together leftover scraps of real amber. This kind of gem is called ambroid. Ambroid looks like the real thing. Buyers of amber must take care to make sure it is real.

Coral

Coral is another gem that can be faked. Plastic, stained bone, and even glass can look like coral. Natural coral has a wood-grain look. Fake coral does not. It is usually solid red or orange in color.

Gold

Scientists can make gold. This gold is no different from natural gold. It costs a lot of money to make, though. It is cheaper to mine natural gold than to make it.

Gems

Man-made gems look like the real thing. They are made in almost the same way that gems form underground. Gem-makers heat powdered minerals to a very high heat. The heat melts the minerals together. Man-made gems can be cut and polished just as natural gems can.

A ring made of imitation gems

Some people also make **imitation** gemstones of glass or crystal. They can also be cut and polished to look like a real gem. In fact, it often takes an expert to see the difference.

Clear stone and glass can be cut to look like diamonds. Some imitation diamonds are man-made. Cubic zirconia is a popular type of man-made diamond. It is hard to tell from the real thing.

The first man-made ruby was formed in 1902. Powdered aluminum oxide and red dye were placed in a blowtorch flame. They melted together and made a gem that looked like a ruby.

Opals can be faked in several ways. Slocum stone is a glass that looks like opal. One kind of fake opal, the Gilson opal, shows a play of colors like a real opal. However, the colors in a Gilson opal look like puzzle pieces.

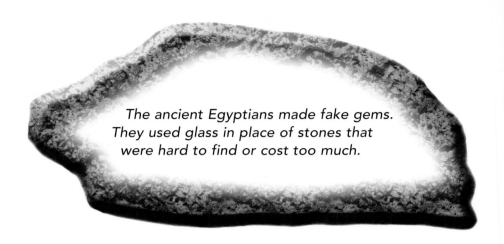

The ancient Egyptians made fake gems. They used glass in place of stones that were hard to find or cost too much.

Some people make imitation opals from a type of plastic. Man-made opals also can be put together from pieces of other opals.

Man-made Gilson turquoise was first made in France in 1972. Fossils are sometimes stained to look like turquoise. Fake turquoise is also made from other gems.

Fossils

Fake fossils are easy to make. People just press fish bones or shells into clay or cement. People also make fake fossils out of plastic.

Glossary

bronze (brahnz) a hard metal made of copper and tin

carats (KAIR uhts) units of weight used to measure gems

crystal (KRIS tuhl) a solid object with flat surfaces that form regular patterns

elements (EHL uh muhnts) substances that cannot be broken down into other kinds of matter

gems (jemz) valuable minerals that have been cut and polished

igneous rock (IHG nee uhs rahk) rock made of hardened lava

imitation (ihm uh TAY shuhn) made to look like something else; not real

industry (IN duhs tree) the work of factories and manufacturing plants

lava (LAH vuh) melted rock that has come up from under the Earth

luster (LUHS tuhr) a soft shine

metamorphic rock (met uh MOHR fik rahk) rock made from other rock that has been squeezed and heated underground

meteorites (MEE tee uh ryts) rocks that have fallen from outer space to Earth

mineral (MIN uhr uhl) a natural solid made of crystals and formed from nonliving materials

nacre (NAY kuhr) the material that lines the inside of shellfish shells

nuggets (NUHG its) small pebbles of metal

ores (ohrz) rocks that contain metals

organics (awr GAN iks) gems made from things that were once alive; nonmineral gems

petrified (PET ruh fyd) turned to rock

precious (PRESH uhs) of great value or high price

resin (REZ uhn) a kind of plant sap or a man-made substance like sap

sediment (SED uh muhnt) small pieces of matter that settle at the bottom of a body of water

sedimentary rock (sed uh MIN tuh ree rahk) rock made from layers of sediment

tarnish (TAHR nish) to lose shine and color because of oxygen in the air

veins (vaynz) long streaks of ore

Index